THE
LAST RIDER

THE FINAL DAYS OF THE PONY EXPRESS

By J. Gunderson

illustrated by José Alfonso Ocampo Ruiz

Librarian Reviewer
Laurie K. Holland
Media Specialist (National Board Certified), Edina, MN
MA in Elementary Education, Minnesota State University, Mankato

Reading Consultant
Elizabeth Stedem
Educator/Consultant, Colorado Springs, CO
MA in Elementary Education, University of Denver, CO

STONE ARCH BOOKS
Minneapolis   San Diego

Graphic Flashbacks are published by Stone Arch Books,
151 Good Counsel Drive, P.O. Box 669,
Mankato, Minnesota 56002.
www.stonearchbooks.com

Library of Congress Cataloging-in-Publication Data
Gunderson, Jessica.
    The Last Rider: The Final Days of the Pony Express / by J. Gunderson; illustrated
by José Alfonso Ocampo Ruiz.
    p. cm. — (Graphic Flash)
    ISBN-13: 978-1-59889-312-0 (library binding)
    ISBN-10: 1-59889-312-2 (library binding)
    ISBN-13: 978-1-59889-407-3 (paperback)
    ISBN-10: 1-59889-407-2 (paperback)
    1. Graphic novels. I. Ocampo Ruiz, José Alfonso. II. Title.
PN6727.G777L37 2007
741.5'973—dc22   2006028033

Summary: Matt Edgars hungers for adventure. The Pony Express is the answer to his
dreams. Riding fast, riding far, he brings the mail to settlers scattered across the Nevada
and Utah deserts. Matt can handle the punishing sun and the poisonous rattlesnakes, but
he's worried about rumors of a war with the Paiute nation. Then someone begins setting
the Express stations on fire. Are these the last days for the young riders?

Art Director: Heather Kindseth
Graphic Designer: Brann Garvey

1 2 3 4 5 6 11 10 09 08 07 06

Printed in the United States of America.

· TABLE OF CONTENTS ·

INTRODUCING . . .

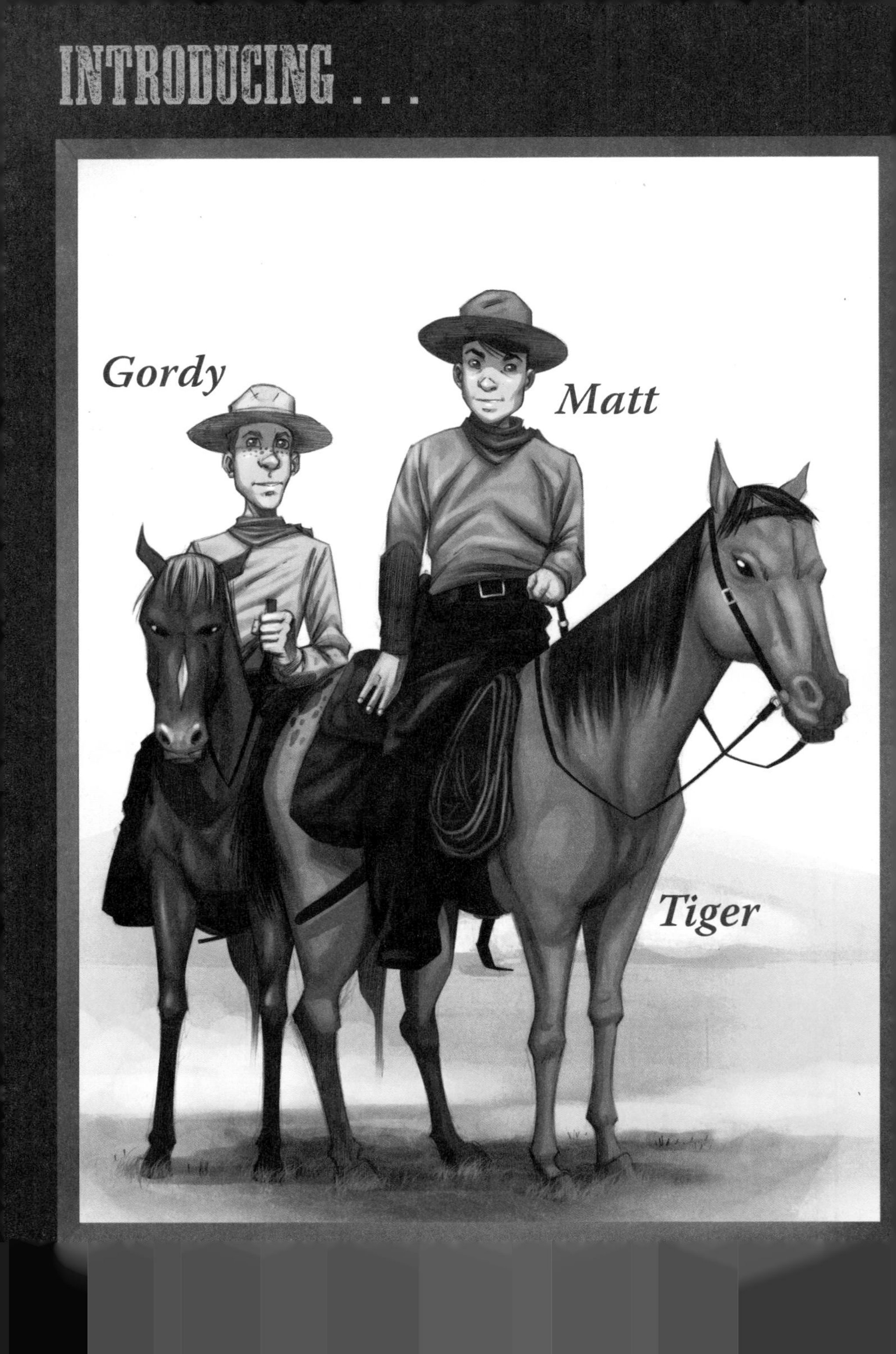

Gordy
Matt
Tiger

Ernie

Tromp

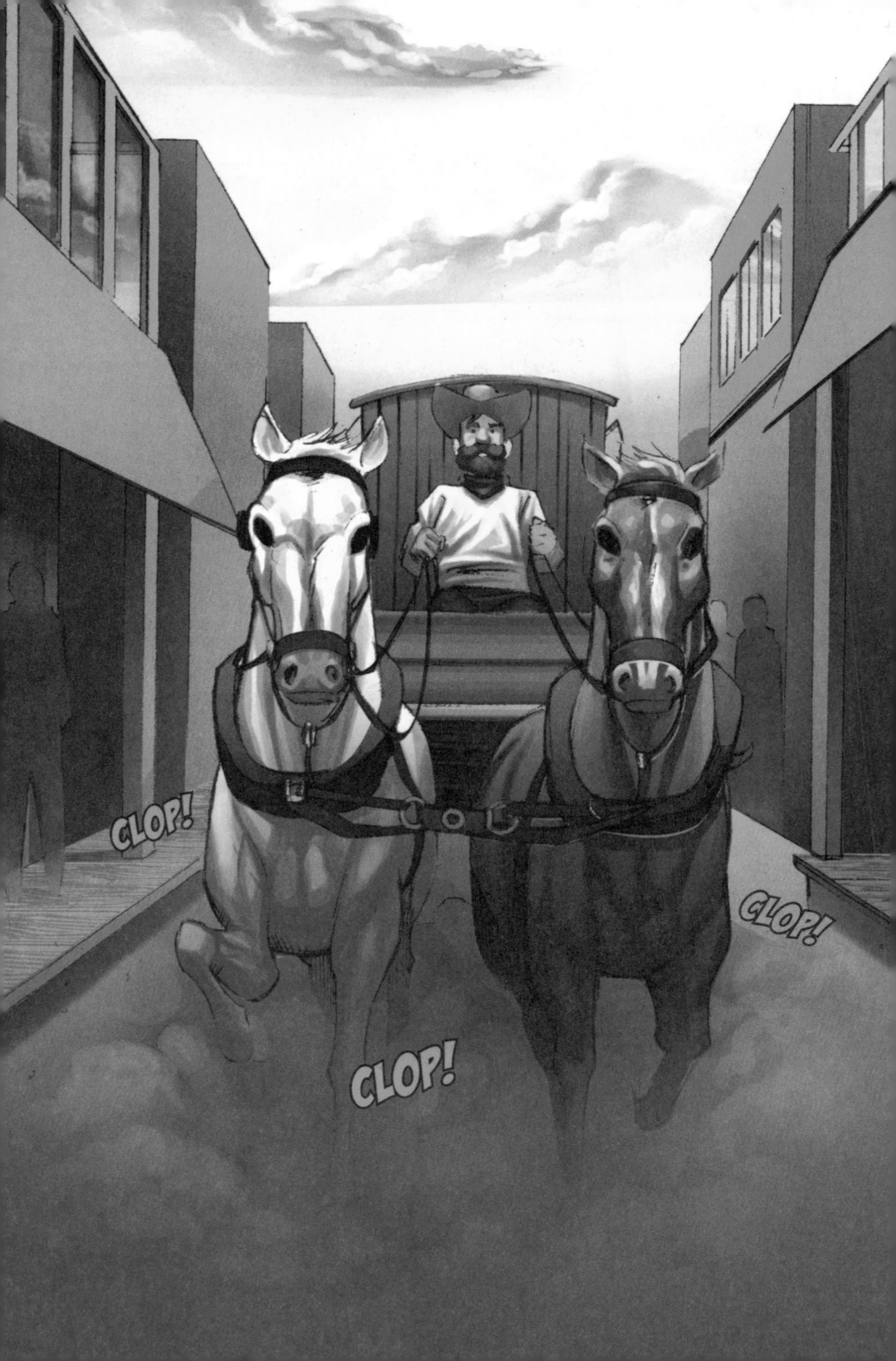
CLOP!
CLOP!
CLOP!

Chapter 1

BRAVE YOUNG RIDERS

Every morning I wake to the sound of horses' hooves on the streets of San Francisco. The hoofbeats remind me of the farm in Kansas where I grew up.

I'd give nearly anything to be back there, helping my father with our horses. But I can never go back. My father died two years ago, in 1858. My mother had to sell our land and all of our horses. Now we live in San Francisco.

City life isn't for me. I ache for open prairies and fields of corn. Most of all, I ache for adventure. I don't know it yet, but this morning my adventure has just begun.

I put on my boots and set out for a quick walk.

That's when I saw the sign. Pony Express! I hurry down to the Express office.

I'm not the only one who longs for adventure. A bunch of other boys, waiting in line, want to ride for the Pony Express, too. Finally it's my turn.

Name?

Matt Edgars.

Age?

I'm sixteen, sir.

"You sure you can handle riding for the Pony Express?" he asks. "It ain't an easy life."

"I can do it, sir," I say. "I know I can."

I spend the next two weeks getting ready. My mom is sad that I'm leaving, but she knows it's time for me to venture out on my own. As I pack my things, I remember something my dad told me right before he died. "Be a hero," he said.

At the time I didn't know what he meant. But now the word repeats over and over in my head. Hero. I like the way it sounds.

Finally the day arrives. I am so excited I'm awake before dawn. I head for the depot and board the train to Nevada. At Carson City, the attendant gives me a horse and points west.

"About a day's ride," he says. "The horse knows the way there."

Nevada is lonelier than I ever imagined. It seems to stretch on forever.

Finally, that night I reach my destination.

I'm surprised by how tired the boys look. I thought Express riders would be brimming over with excitement and energy. These boys just look plain exhausted.

Ernie doesn't notice my disappointment. He starts explaining my duties.

"You'll be riding three days a week between Stone Creek and Yellow Sands station," he says. "Your route is eighty miles long. You'll change horses along the way, but you won't have time for rest during your route. Ride as fast as you can. Got that?"

"Fast as I can," I say. "Yes, sir." The Pony Express doesn't sound like an adventure. It sounds like work.

"Your duty is to carry the mail. And my name's Ernie, not sir! Don't forget it, kid."

"I won't, sir," I say, then realize my mistake. The other boys laugh. Over his shoulder he says, "Now get some sleep. You ride first thing in the morning."

Chapter 2
FIRST RIDE

Before I know it, I'm standing in the cold morning, waiting for my turn to ride. Who'd have thought the desert could make you shiver?

"You have two minutes to get the mochila onto your horse," says Ernie. "The mochila is the pouch that holds the mail."

Suddenly, I hear Gordy, one of the other boys, yell out: "Rider coming!"

"You ready?" asks Ernie.

"Ready as ever!" I say.

"Careful, boy," Ernie tells me. "Your horse, Tiger, is a wild one!"

Great, I say to myself. Now he tells me!

With only a small pistol and a canteen of water by my side, I begin my first ride.

We gallop through the brush, over hills, and through streams.

By sunup I'm soaked with sweat. So is Tiger.

And so I ride on into the afternoon. I don't see a single soul except the station keepers. Nevada really is as empty as I've heard. I feel like I'm the only person under the sun.

Tiger and I splash through a cool stream. Up ahead, I see a small station. "That looks like the next station, Tiger. That's where you and I say farewell," I tell my trusty horse.

We trot up to the station, where the station keeper stands, holding the reins of the new horse. "Any troubles?" he asks.

"Nope. All's well," I say, mounting the horse.

"Good," he says as I ride away. "I've been worried."

"About what?" I call back.

"Never mind," he says.

The new horse and I trot through a gully, thick with shrubbery. The sun is hot. I'm so tired, I have to use all my strength to hold onto the reins.

In the afternoon, the sunlight slips out of the gully. The cool shadows feel good.

I think I must have started to doze when I hear a strange noise.

I tell myself that it is just a wild animal in the brush. But I can't shake the feeling that something, or someone, is watching me.

Chapter 3

THE MYSTERY OF BILLY BURNS

"My name's Tom, but you can call me Tromp," the station keeper says. I follow Tromp inside the station. He scoops up a plate of beans and cornbread and hands it to me. "This is all I've got," he says.

"It's delicious," I say between bites. "Thanks." I've never liked beans, but today I'm hungry enough to eat a cactus.

Without taking his eyes off my plate, Tromp says, "You must be taking over Billy Burns' route. Poor Billy."

I look at him, with my forkful of beans halfway to my open mouth.

"Whatever happened to him?" I say.

"Eat all you want, kid," Tromp tells me.

Then he gets up and starts walking away. "And get some rest. You've got another ride tomorrow."

I lie down in the bunk in the corner, but I can't fall asleep. My mind is whirling like a prairie tornado.

I keep remembering the sounds I heard back in that gully. And most of all, I wonder about the last rider. Why won't Tromp tell me?

What happened to Billy Burns?

The next morning Tromp is awake before the sun erases the stars. I pull myself from bed even though my muscles are screaming with pain. I gulp some coffee and am ready when the next rider tosses me the mochila.

"Careful, kid," Tromp hollers after me.

The bright sun has lifted my spirits. When I reach Stone Creek, I get a funny feeling I never expected. It feels like coming home.

But I still can't forget about Billy Burns.

Later that night, we're all in our bunks, staring at the ceiling and talking about our lives back home. I get up the nerve to say what is on my mind. "What ever happened to the last rider? The one I'm replacing?"

"I don't think we should tell," whispers Hank.

"The kid should know," says Gordy. Then he turns on his creaking bunk and faces me. "Billy Burns was killed," he says.

KILLED?

"Quiet in there, boys!" Ernie yells.

I have three days until my next ride. Instead of resting, I decide to help Ernie with the horses.

"See anything on your first ride?" Ernie asks me. "Anything suspicious?"

"The Paiute Indians who live here don't like us," says Ernie.

Ernie explains that as more and more settlers head west, more and more land is being taken from the Paiutes. White settlers chop down timber the Paiutes need for firewood. They also hunt animals the Paiutes use for food.

So why don't folks just stop settling here?" I ask.

"Most people think they can live anywhere they want," says Ernie.

The conflict between the settlers and the Paiute Indians doesn't surprise me. All over the West, settlers are fighting the Indian tribes for control of the land.

"Does this have anything to do with Billy Burns getting killed?" I ask.

"Billy was killed by someone," says Ernie, carefully. "Everyone thinks it was the Paiutes. But I have my own theory about what happened."

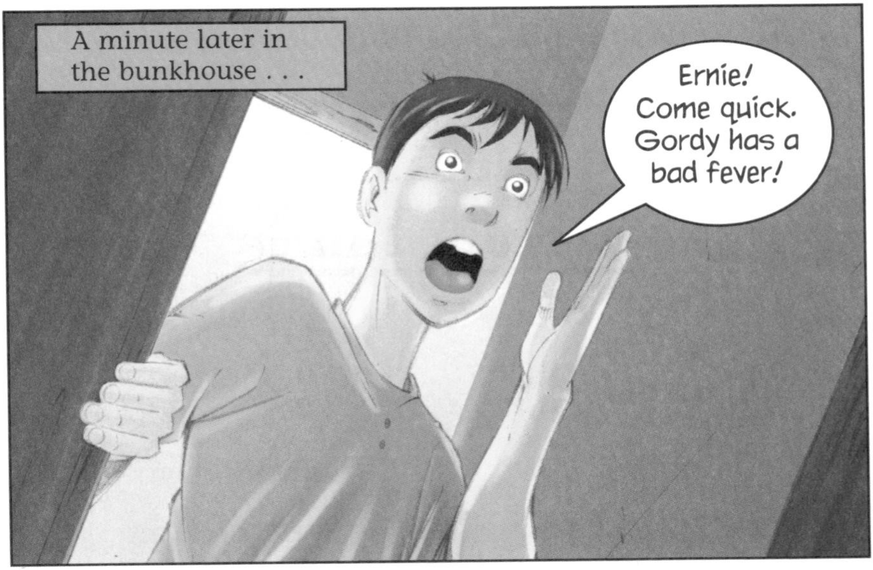
A minute later in the bunkhouse . . .
Ernie! Come quick. Gordy has a bad fever!

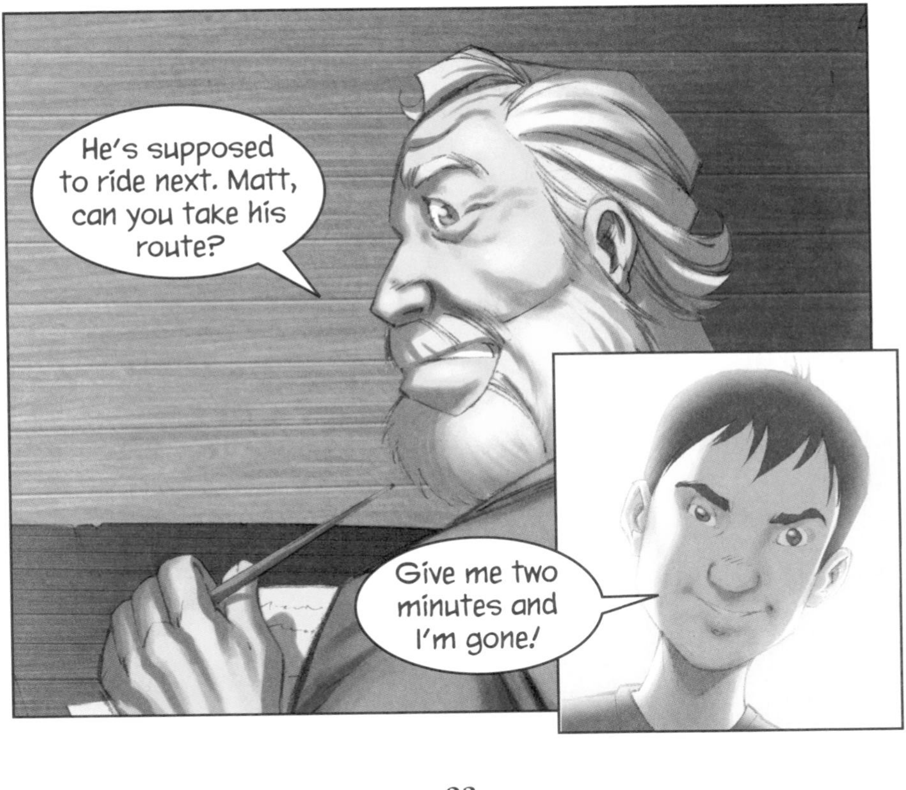
He's supposed to ride next. Matt, can you take his route?
Give me two minutes and I'm gone!

Chapter 4

FIRE AT YELLOW SANDS

The next morning, when the rider gallops into the station, it is a kid I have never seen before. He looks young, maybe even thirteen.

"Everything okay?" I ask.

The kid almost falls out of his saddle. He eyes are droopy with sleep.

"So far so good," he says. "But the station keepers are worried about the Paiutes. Be careful."

I swing up onto the saddle. "Thanks," I tell him. "I'll keep my eyes peeled."

So I'm off on my next ride. Even though things look calm, I stay alert to every sound.

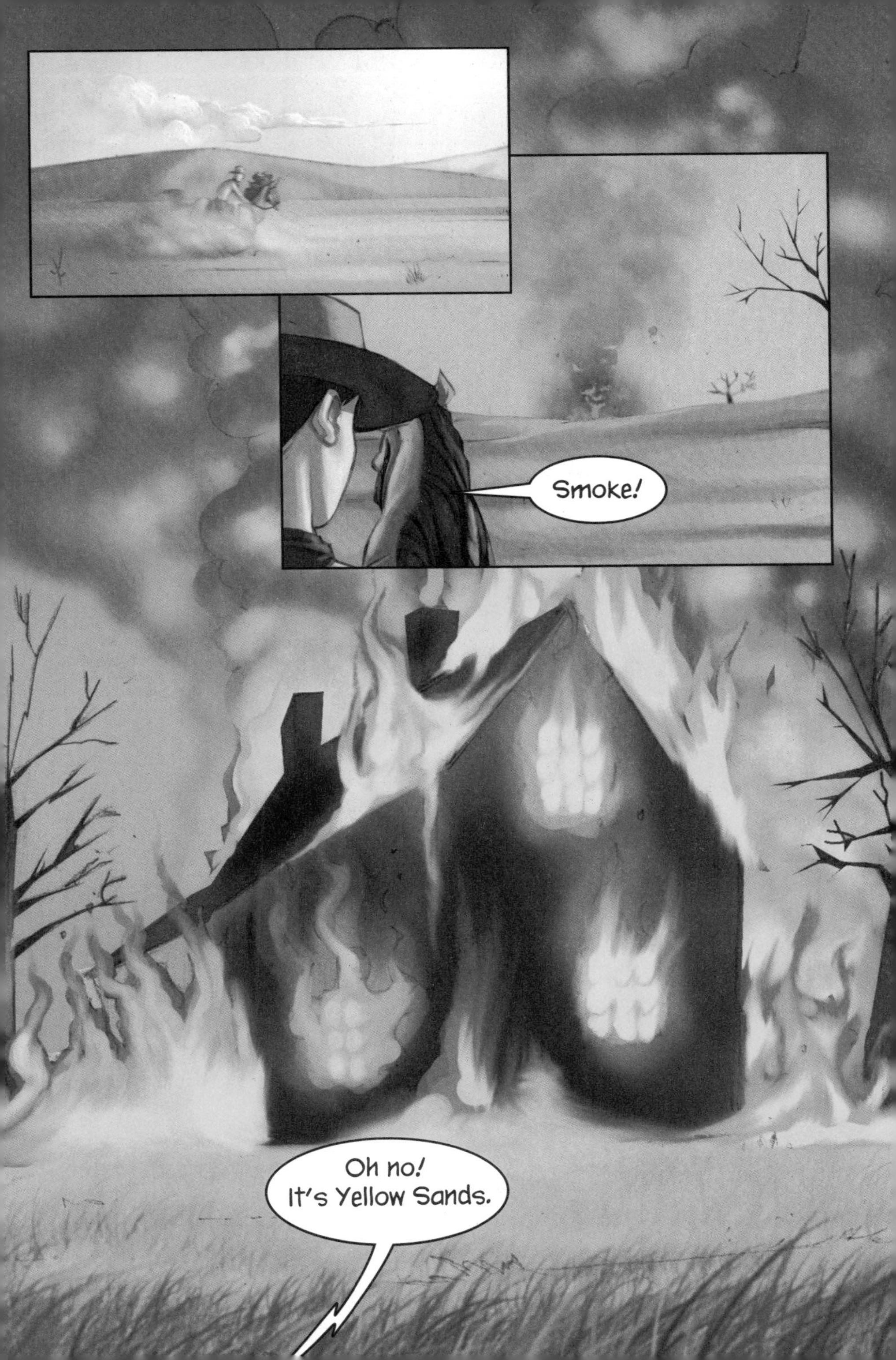
Smoke!
Oh no! It's Yellow Sands.

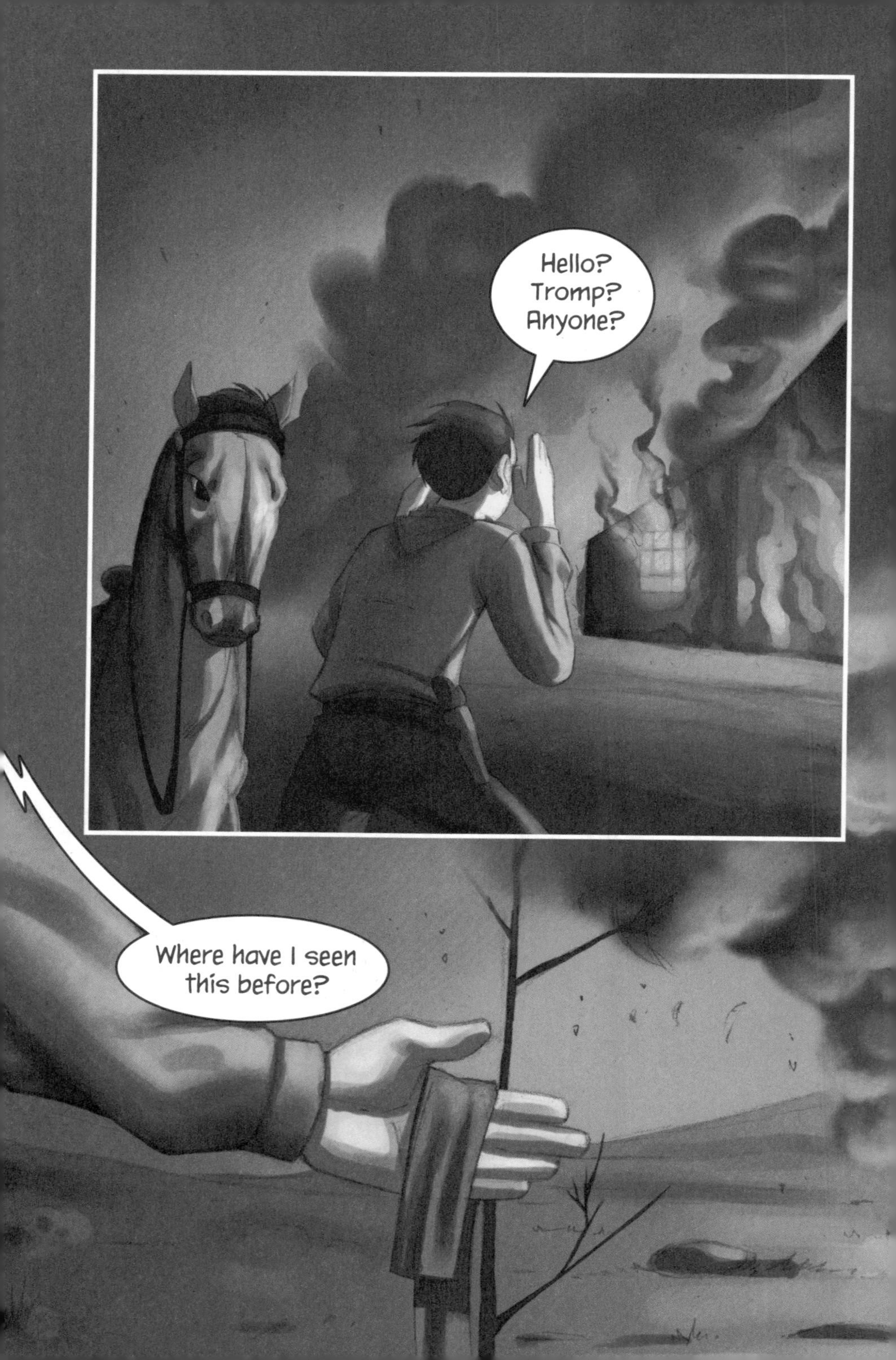
Hello? Tromp? Anyone?
Where have I seen this before?

I don't know if the Paiutes did this or not. I do know that I better get to the next station and warn them, just in case.

As I approach the next station, I can see the keeper is holding a rifle.

"Whoa, it's me," I yell. "Pony Express!"

I can see another man looking out a window at me. He's holding a rifle, too.

The station keeper runs up to greet me as I rein in my horse.

"There's been a fire at Yellow Sands," I tell him.

"We've heard," the man says. "Tromp and the others escaped and came here."

"What happened?" I ask.

"It's those Paiute Indians," he says. "War is on!"

Then the station keeper tells me there has been a battle between American soldiers and the Paiute Indians at nearby Pyramid Lake.

"I advise you to giddy-up back to Stone Creek as fast as you can go, son."

"What about the mail?" I ask.

"I've got a rider inside who's gonna take it. Now, get!"

War!

I'd been longing for adventure before, but not this kind.

I just don't understand.

"If the Indians don't want us here," I say, "then why don't we leave?"

The station keeper looks at me as if I am a rattlesnake that just crawled out from a rock.

"You're crazy, kid," he says. "I've never heard such an idea."

It makes sense to me, I think.

Then the man in the window yells out at me. "You better get out of here, boy!"

I ride all night, spreading the news of the Paiute War at every station that dots my route. By the time I reach Stone Creek, the morning sun is a small red blossom on the horizon.

Ernie had already heard about the fire and the Paiutes. Bad news travels fast on the Pony Express. But when I go inside, ready for a rest after my long night, I see something that is even worse news.

The boys are leaving! They're stuffing their bags full of clothes. All the boys that is, except for Gordy. He's still sick, lying on his bunk in the corner.

"What's going on?" I say

"I'm getting out of here," says Hank.

"I ain't risking my life just to carry a piece of someone else's mail," says Jed.

"But what about our duty?" I say. "Who's going to take the mail?"

"Someone else can have my duty," says Jed.

What about our job? What about all the work we've already done?

The boys grab their bags and hats and head outside to their saddled horses. A big shadow appears in the doorway. It's Ernie.

"Well, Matt," he says in a quiet voice. "What are you going to do?"

"I'm staying," I say. "I made a promise to the Pony Express and I plan on keeping it."

Ernie doesn't smile. I've never seen him smile. But he lets out a big sigh of relief. It smells of baked beans.

"I hope you know what you're in for, kid," he says.

I know that if my father could see me now,
he'd be proud of me. I hear his words again.
"Be a hero."

Chapter 5

PAIUTE

Days pass, and there isn't a single rider in sight. It seems like everyone on the Pony Express has quit. But we know that somewhere, mail is being sent. And I'm the one who will help carry it.

Ernie and I keep watch, rifles in hand, ready for any sign of trouble.

I stand on the steps of the station house and shade my eyes with my hand. I can see something hanging on the side of the horse. A mochila! It's a Pony Express rider.

"About time," says Ernie. Then he turns to me. "Gordy's still not well enough. You ready to ride, Matt?"

"Let me just fill my canteen," I say, "and then I'm ready."

In a few minutes, the other rider is off his horse and helps me place the mochila on Tiger.

The rider looks me squarely in the face.

"No one wants to ride in these parts," he says.

I reckon the Pony Express is about to call it quits.

I ride away, my mind churning as fast as Tiger's hooves. Could this be my final ride?

Tiger and I stay at a steady pace. I have no idea what lies ahead. Maybe there are no station keepers up ahead. Maybe no one will be willing to ride. I might have to ride for days.

I'll do whatever it takes to get the mail through, I think. Even if I have to ride through the middle of a war!

Under the hot sun, my mind wanders. I think about Billy Burns. Was he killed by Paiutes? Am I about to suffer the same fate?

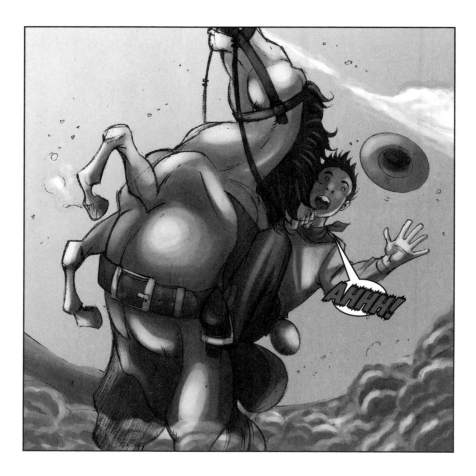

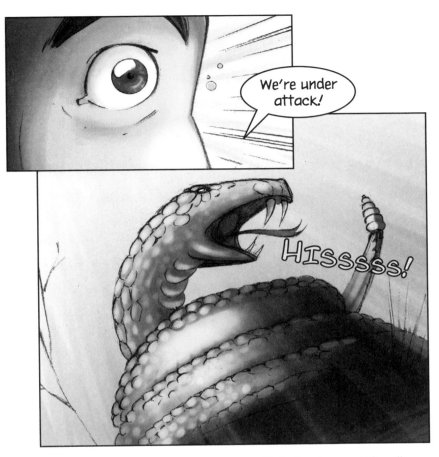

"Easy, girl," I say to Tiger. "It's just a rattler."

Paiute attacks I can't handle, but snakes I can. I ease Tiger away from the rattlesnake, one step at a time. Sweat is running down my back, and it's not from the morning sun.

Relief sweeps over me. For a second there, I thought I was a goner for sure.

From now on, I'll have to stay alert. I can't let my mind wander.

After our scare with the rattler, Tiger is scared by every sound. I use the tricks my father taught me to calm her. I smooth her mane and let her nibble on a piece of bread.

Then I see a sight in the distance that makes the hair on my neck stand up straight.

I look right and
left. There is no
route around them.

I have to ride
past them if I want
to continue with
the mail.

Their arrows glint in the sun. I move slowly
toward the trio.

What will happen next?

Will I end up like Billy Burns?

The warriors watch me carefully.

As I ride up the ridge, a thought strikes me. I
want the Paiute to know I don't want their land.
I am just a rider passing through.

I need to show these men that I mean them
no harm.

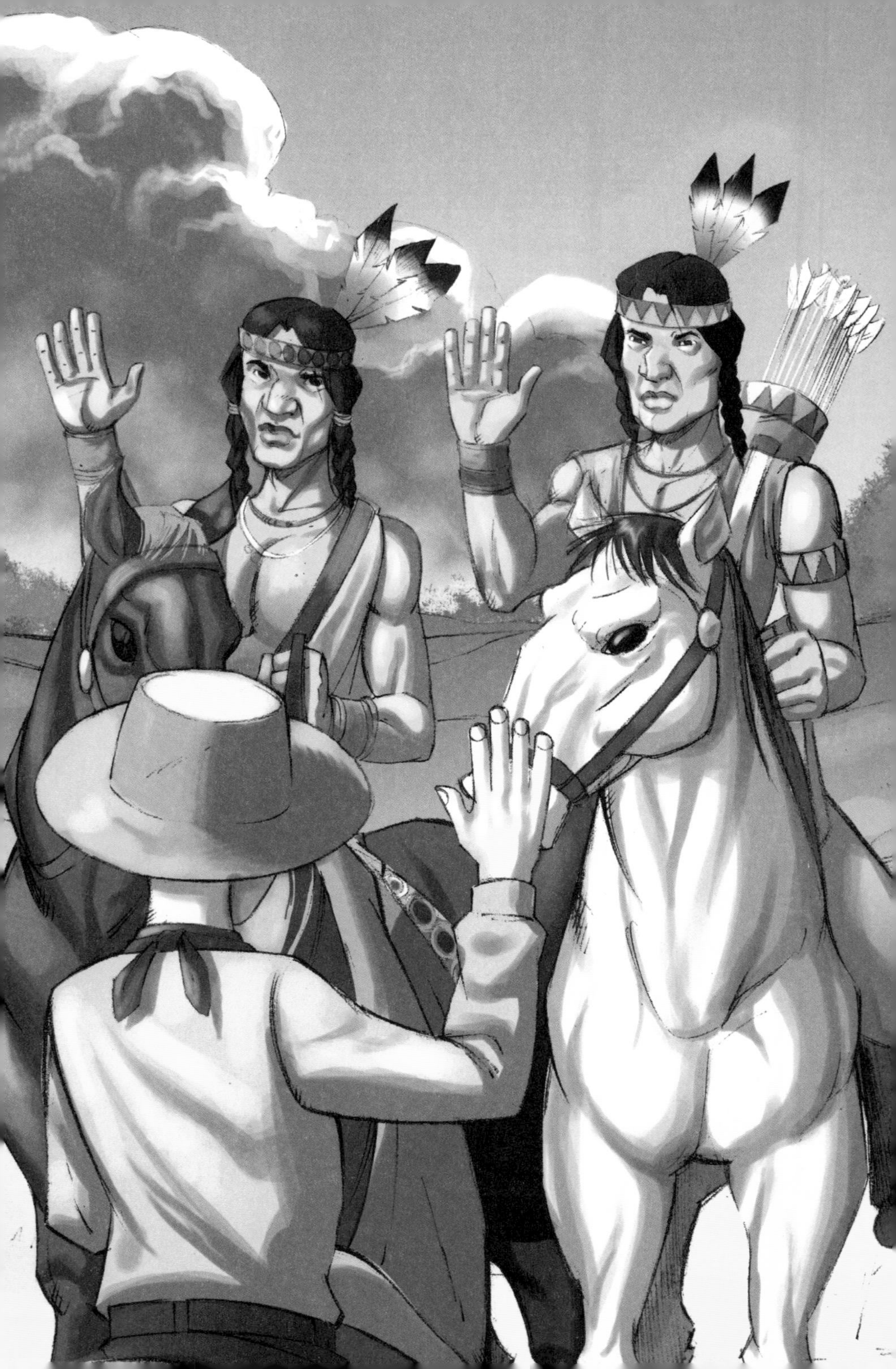

Whew! I breathe a sigh of relief as I pass the Paiutes. They make no move, but they are watching me steadily.

After we reach the top of the ridge, I urge Tiger to a gallop. We fly down the hill. I crouch low in my saddle and don't look back.

I reach the next station in record time. I tell the station keeper about my scare with the Paiutes. He listens to my story, and then says, "Some of my boys are signing up to fight the Indians. You in?"

"My duty is with the Pony Express," I say. "I don't want to fight."

The station keeper nods. He tells me to get some rest. Tomorrow I'll head back to Stone Creek.

As I drift off to sleep, I hear my father's voice. "You're a hero, Matt," he says.

Chapter 6

THE BANDANA BANDITS

The next day, Tiger and I are rested and ready to return to Stone Creek. I brush her coat and let her drink water from my hand.

"You saved me yesterday," I tell her. "If you weren't so fast and wild, girl, we might have been goners."

I saddle up and begin the ride to my home station. I'm on the lookout for danger, but the only sign of life I see is a hawk flying high above us.

As we near Stone Creek, I hear shouts.

Tiger quickens her speed without my urging. What's going on? Is something happening to Ernie and Gordy?

I see four strange men on horses in front of the station. They have bright red bandanas tied around their faces.

Bandits!

Their horses are scattering and rearing.

"Come on, Tiger!" I yell.

One of the men is galloping toward me.

"Stop him, Matt!" yells Gordy.

The horseman is almost past me. I can see the frightened eyes of his horse.

I remember my days back in Kansas. My hand goes to my rope, as I quickly pull it loose from the saddle.

As the man hits the dirt, the wind is knocked out of him. I quickly dismount, keeping hold of my end of the rope. Then I squat down and truss up the man's hands behind his back. This guy ain't going anywhere.

"I'm taking you back to the station," I say. "You have some explaining to do."

"I ain't telling you nothing," the man spits out.

I don't want to believe him, but as we approach the building, it looks silent and deserted.

Fear spreads over me. Could Ernie and Gordy be dead?

"Man! I thought you were goners," I say.

"We were busy rounding up these other fellows," says Ernie. We send Gordy to fetch a sheriff from a nearby town. As we're waiting for the lawman, I ask Ernie, "Who are these men?"

The man I caught answers me. "You've never heard of us, boy?"

I shake my head no.

"Not many people have," says Ernie. "That's because they like to wear disguises."

He reaches into a canvas bag near his feet and pulls out an arrow, feathers, and a leather shirt.

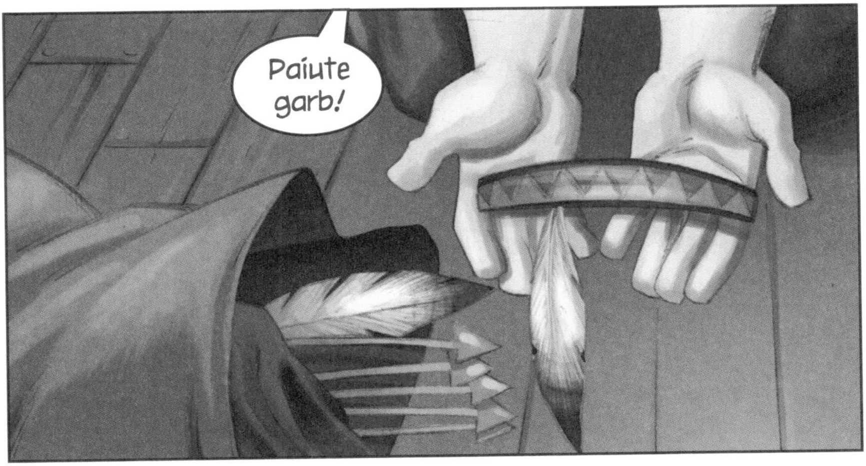
Paiute garb!

Ernie chuckles. "I knew it wasn't the Paiutes!" he says. "My hunch was right!"

I look at the men's red bandanas. I remember the ones I saw in the gully and at Yellow Sands.

"They've been leaving their calling card behind," I tell Ernie.

Soon Gordy arrives with the sheriff's men. They load the gang into a wagon.

"They're going to jail for a long time," the sheriff promises.

"Ask them if they had anything to do with a rider named Billy Burns," I say.

Then the sheriff tells us some disturbing news. The Pony Express will be stopping service in Nevada until the war with the Paiutes is over.

"I hear they need riders in Kansas," the sheriff says.

Ernie looks at me with a wink. "Kansas?" Then he turns to the sheriff and says, "I got a good friend who comes from Kansas. Maybe I'll go there and visit him for a spell."

After the lawmen leave with the bandits, Ernie and Gordy and I look at the station house. We won't be seeing it ever again.

"You were sure good with that lasso,"
says Gordy.

"You were a real hero today, Matt," says Ernie.

I smooth my horse's mane. "Don't forget
Tiger," I say. "I couldn't have done it without her.
We're a team."

ABOUT THE AUTHOR

Jessica Gunderson grew up in the small town of Washburn, North Dakota. She has a bachelor's degree from the University of North Dakota and a master's degree in creative writing from Minnesota State University, Mankato. She likes rainy days and thunderstorms. She also likes exploring haunted houses and playing MadLibs. She teaches English in Madison, Wisconsin, where she lives with her cat, Yossarian.

GLOSSARY

canteen (kan-TEEN)—a small container for holding water or other liquids

conflict (KON-flikt)—a war or a period of fighting

courage (KUR-ij)—bravery or fearlessness

delirious (di-LEER-ee-uhss)—unable to think straight because of a fever

depot (DEE-poh)—a station along the Pony Express trailway

disappointment (diss-uh-POYNT-mehnt)—the feeling of being let down

exhausted (eg-ZAWST-ed)—very tired

mochila (moh-CHEE-la)—a bag with several pockets designed to fit over a saddle, used by Pony Express riders to carry mail

Paiute (pye-YOOT)—a group of Native Americans who lived in Utah and Nevada

protect (pruh-TEKT)—to keep something safe from harm

theory (THEER-ee)—an idea based on some evidence but not proven

THE PONY EXPRESS

The Pony Express carried mail between St. Joseph, Missouri and Sacramento, California. A trip one way would take about ten days. Each rider had a route of about 80 miles and changed horses ten times on his route.

The war with the Paiute lasted about one month. During the war, many Pony Express stations in Nevada were destroyed.

During the settling of the West, many wars were fought between American Indians and U.S. soldiers. By the end of the 1800's, settlers had taken over most of the American Indians' land. Indians were forced to move onto reservations. Many of them died because of war and disease brought by white settlers.

The Civil War between the North and South started in April, 1861. Pony Express riders carried news of the war to western states. The quick communication between the eastern and western states helped California and Oregon stay in the Union.

President Abraham Lincoln's Inaugural Address in March, 1861, was the fastest-traveling piece of mail delivered by the Pony Express. It was delivered in 7 days and 17 hours.

The Pony Express lasted only 1½ years. It began in April 1860 and ended in October 1861. The Express was replaced by a new invention, the telegraph. Telegraphs sent messages along wires in seconds using Morse code and electrical signals.

DISCUSSION QUESTIONS

1. At the end of the story, Ernie called Matt a "hero." When you hear the word "hero, who do you think of? What makes someone a hero?

2. Why do you think Matt chose to stay with Ernie at Stone Creek instead of leaving with the other boys?

3. The United States often fought wars with the American Indians in order to gain control of their land. The United States was growing and needed more land to settle on. What other choices besides war did the U.S. have?

WRITING PROMPTS

1. Pretend you are a Pony Express rider. You have to ride for three days all alone. How would you keep cool during a hot ride? What would you do to help stay awake? Write and describe what it's like to be an Express rider.

2. Matt decided to stay with the Pony Express. What might have happened if he had decided to leave instead? Write and describe what would happen to Matt.

3. The Paiute Indians were accused of robbery and kidnapping. Some of these crimes they did not commit. Have you ever accused someone of something he or she didn't do? Describe what happened and how you felt.

INTERNET SITES

Do you want to know more about subjects related to this book? Or are you interested in learning about other topics? Then check out FactHound, a fun, easy way to find Internet sites.

Our investigative staff has already sniffed out great sites for you!

Here's how to use FactHound:

1. Visit *www.facthound.com*

2. Select your grade level.

3. To learn more about subjects related to this book, type in the book's ISBN number: **159883122**.

4. Click the **Fetch It** button.

FactHound will fetch the best Internet sites for you.